Mr. and Mrs. Portly and Their Little Dog, Snack

SANDRA JORDAN Pictures by CHRISTINE DAVENIER

FARRAR STRAUS GIROUX
NEW YORK

Mrs. Amanda Portly didn't want a dog, not one bit, but when she looked into Snack's hopeful brown eyes she just couldn't help herself.

"You need a good home. I have a good home. How lucky is that?" she said.

She scooped him into her grocery basket between the ripe garden tomatoes and crookneck squash. "Look out for the watermelon," she warned him. "It keeps rolling around."

Snack lifted his paws and put them firmly on the melon.

"Is he the smartest thing you ever saw?" said Mrs. Portly to the cashier. "I can't wait till Mr. Portly gets back from his fishing trip. He'll be so surprised!"

"Does Mr. Portly like dogs?" asked the cashier.

"Well, Zander Portly can be quite persnickety, but I'm sure he will," said Mrs. Portly, "once he gets used to the idea."

At home Mrs. Portly sat Snack on the kitchen counter for a serious talk. "These are the rules," she told him.

"Don't bark before Mr. Portly wakes up.

"Don't chew Mr. Portly's shoes.

"Don't drink out of Mr. Portly's toilet.

"Don't get hair on Mr. Portly's suits.

"And never, ever put so much as a paw in the living room. The paintings in there are world famous, and Mr. Portly is extra-specially persnickety about them. Why, we have *Landscape* by Phizzer, *Seascape* by Bruzzer, and even *Portrait* by Kline. The Kline is a truly important work."

"*Yip, yip, yip,*" said Snack, and licked Mrs. Portly's hand to show that he loved rules, he loved art, and, most of all, he loved her.

She said, "Oh, who is a good dog? Who is he? My Snackie-boo." Without a doubt, Mrs. Portly already loved Snack, too.

The next morning after breakfast, Snack followed Mrs. Portly into the sunroom, where she had her own painting studio. Amanda Portly was not as famous as Phizzer, Bruzzer, and Kline–not yet–but in Snack's opinion her paintings were far better than theirs. He stood at attention, ready to work.

"What do you think, Snack? Should I make the vase yellow or green?"

"*Gr-r-r-r,*" said Snack.

"Green it is," said Mrs. Portly. "Now, should I make the flowers red or purple?"

"*R-r-r-r,*" said Snack, and Mrs. Portly covered her canvas with every shade of red paint. "Thank you, Snack. I believe in this painting we've captured the true spirit of red dahlias. You have been an amazing help to me."

Mrs. Portly screwed the tops on her tubes of paint and cleaned her brushes. Then she and Snack ate their dinner.

After dinner, he sat cozily at her feet while they watched television—the evening news for Mrs. Portly, followed by cartoons for Snack.

At last, they turned out the lights and went upstairs. Mrs. Portly read for a while, but Snack snuggled down on Mr. Portly's pillow and went right to sleep.

With Snack at her side, Mrs. Portly was inspired. That week, paintings sprang from her brush. She saved the first one, *Red Dahlias in a Green Vase*, but the rest she proudly took downtown to Mr. B., who occasionally displayed her work in his gallery. Mr. B. bought them all and pleaded for more. With part of the money he paid her, she bought Snack a shiny blue leash to wear when they walked around the neighborhood.

By Sunday night, when Mr. Portly pulled into the driveway and unloaded his fishing rods, Mrs. Portly and Snack were a team.

"Look what I bought for you, Zander," said Mrs. Portly. "A darling puppy."

"Puppies grow up to be dogs," said Mr. Portly. "I hate dogs."

"Oh, you don't mean that," said Mrs. Portly. "Look at his sweet face."

But Mr. Portly did mean it. "I like art," he said. "I like beauty. Dogs shed. Dogs chew. Dogs lick."

"Sh-h-h! You'll hurt his feelings. He's very intelligent. Why, he helps me with my paintings. I sold four of them, and I saved a special one for you, Zander. What do you think?"

"Amazing," said Mr. Portly. "You've captured the true spirit of red dahlias, Amanda."

"That's exactly what I hoped you'd say," said Mrs. Portly.

"We'll hang it in the living room tonight." Mr. Portly kissed Mrs. Portly and glared fiercely at Snack.

Snack tried to make friends with Mr. Portly, but every day Mr. Portly hated Snack more. "Amanda! Look at my chair. Look what he did to my chair."

"Only dog hair," said Mrs. Portly. "You can brush it right off."

"He chewed my paper. I can't read the news."

"He fetched it for you. Isn't he a clever boy? We can watch the news on television, Zander. And I'll let you tickle my back."

"Well, all right," said Mr. Portly, less grumpy. He loved to tickle Mrs. Portly's back.

Snack lay sadly in a corner. No more sitting cozily at Mrs. Portly's dainty feet. No more cartoons. "Absolutely not," said Mr. Portly, and that was that. And worst of all, he had to sleep in his own bed instead of with Mrs. Portly. Mr. Portly wouldn't even let him in the bedroom!

Snack knew Mrs. Portly loved him. But how could he ever win Mr. Portly's persnickety heart?

He jumped up and licked Mr. Portly's face to welcome him home from the office.

He dug up his favorite chewy bone and left it in Mr. Portly's slipper, where he would be sure to find it.

Nothing worked.

Snack grew desperate. That very night, after his evening walk, he marched into the living room and boldly gazed at the Phizzer, the Bruzzer, and the Kline. Surely Mr. Portly would appreciate a dog who shared his taste in art.

That was his biggest mistake of all.

"Muddy paw prints! In the living room!" roared Mr. Portly. "That's it. The dog goes . . . or I go."

Mrs. Portly pondered her decision.

Snack helped her with her paintings.

But Mr. Portly proudly hung one of them in the living room right next to the Phizzer, the Bruzzer, and the Kline.

Snack sat at her feet while they watched television.

But Mr. Portly tickled her back.

Snack snored in a restful way.

But so did Mr. Portly.

How could she choose? She loved them both.

Mr. Portly grew nervous watching Mrs. Portly think. "All right, then," he grouched. "If it's so important to you, he can stay. But we're getting a doghouse. Dogs belong outside."

So Mrs. Portly bought Snack an absolutely stupendous doghouse. "It's only for a little while," she whispered to him. "Mr. Portly was born persnickety, and he'll die persnickety. But he has a good, kind heart. In time, he'll come around. You'll see."

Snack's new house was the wonder of the neighborhood, but he took no joy in it, not even when Mrs. Portly planted dahlia beds on three sides of the house in his favorite shade of red.

During the day, she always brought Snack into the sunroom to sit by her easel. But Snack felt too sad to bark suggestions. Yards were fine for some dogs, but he was an indoor dog, an art-loving dog. He wanted to sit with Mrs. Portly and watch cartoons. Why didn't Mr. Portly understand that?

At bedtime, Mrs. Portly came out to the doghouse to give him a kiss and say good night. Then Snack hopefully watched her bedroom window. If Mr. Portly had that change of heart, Snack didn't want to miss a minute of it. Only when the light went out did he fall into restless sleep.

One evening, just as Snack dozed off, he heard the crash and tinkle of glass breaking. He put his head out the door of his doghouse. A Bad Man was breaking the glass of the French doors to the living room and reaching in to unlock them. If Mr. Portly saw him, he would be angry. But Mr. Portly was asleep upstairs with Mrs. Portly. Snack watched the Bad Man creep through the unlocked French doors and enter the house.

He saw him take *Landscape* by Phizzer off the wall and put it into his big black bag. Snack yawned.

Seascape by Bruzzer followed the Phizzer into the bag. Snack stretched.

Then the Bad Man took down *Portrait* by Kline and put it into the bag, too. Snack scratched an itchy place behind his ear.

The Bad Man started to tiptoe out of the house. But wait–he opened his big black bag once more. Into it he put Mrs. Portly's painting of *Red Dahlias in a Green Vase.* The first one she and Snack had done together.

Snack leaped to his feet. *"Arf, arf, arf. Roof, roof, roof. Aroo-ooo. Aroo-ooo-ooo!"*

The Bad Man ran out of the house carrying the big black bag. "Be quiet," he hissed. "Good dog. Be quiet."

"*Gr-r-r-r,*" growled Snack, and then he opened his mouth as wide as it would go and bit the Bad Man's nasty leg.

"Let go, you rotten mutt," said the Bad Man. He dropped the bag and ran for his life.

Mr. and Mrs. Portly came rushing outside. While Mr. Portly chased the Bad Man yelling "Stop, thief!" Mrs. Portly hugged Snack.

"What a good, good boy," she said. "My little Snackie-wackel."

Then Mr. Portly came trudging back. "He got away," he said. "The paintings are gone. All gone."

"But you're safe, my brave Zander," said Mrs. Portly. "That's what's important."

"And so are you," said Mr. Portly, clasping her to his chest. "My dear Amanda."

"And don't forget our hero, Snack," said Mrs. Portly.

"Ah, Snack," said Mr. Portly, and he actually reached down and scratched Snack right under his furry chin.

"Arf," said Snack. And then, to show he bore Mr. Portly no grudge, he led them to the dahlia bed. There were all the paintings, safe and sound.

"Now, isn't he the best Snackie you ever met?" said Mrs. Portly.

"I guess he is," said Mr. Portly.

"And don't you love him to death?" said Mrs. Portly.

"I guess I do," said Mr. Portly.

"And no more doghouse, ever," said Mrs. Portly.

"I guess not," said Mr. Portly.

With Mrs. Portly and Snack helping, Mr. Portly rehung all the paintings. Then Snack joyfully followed Mr. and Mrs. Portly up the stairs.

"He sleeps in his own bed," said Mr. Portly.

"Of course he will. Whatever makes you happy, dear."

For all my dog-nutty friends and relatives–including Barbara; Eileen; Jan and Ronnie; John Chris, Ellen, and Jack; Linda and Chris; Maggie; Mark; Nancie; Samantha, Allie, and Lucy; Sasha; Scottie-boy and Kim. This story absolutely is not about you guys. Scout's honor. –S.J.

For our dear friend Edmund White and our adorable Fred. –C.D.

Distributed in Canada by Douglas & McIntyre Ltd.
Color separations by Chroma Graphics PTE Ltd.
Printed in February 2009 in China by South China Printing Company Ltd., Dongguan City, Guangdong Province
Designed by Robbin Gourley
First edition, 2009
10 9 8 7 6 5 4 3 2 1

www.fsgkidsbooks.com

Library of Congress Cataloging-in-Publication Data
Jordan, Sandra, date.
Mr. and Mrs. Portly and their little dog Snack / Sandra Jordan ; pictures by Christine Davenier.– 1st ed.
p. cm.
Summary: Snack is a very happy puppy when Mrs. Portly adopts him but when persnickety Mr. Portly returns from a fishing trip, he banishes Snack to a doghouse until their mutual love of art, and a thief, bring them together.
ISBN-13: 978-0-374-35089-5
ISBN-10: 0-374-35089-2
[1. Human-animal relationships–Fiction. 2. Dogs–Fiction. 3. Animals–Infancy–Fiction. 4. Art–Fiction.] I. Davenier, Christine, ill. II. Title.

PZ7.J7683 Mr 2009
[E]–dc22

2007046663